D1395309

To Thomas

Text and illustrations copyright © 1981 by Jenny Partridge
Published by World's Work Ltd
The Windmill Press, Kingswood, Tadworth, Surrey
Layout and design by The Romany Studio Workshop
Reproduced by Graphic Affairs Ltd, Southend
Printed in Great Britain by
William Clowes (Beccles) Limited, Beccles and London
Second impression 1982
SBN 437 66178 4

Harriet Plume

JENNY PARTRIDGE

A WORLD'S WORK CHILDREN'S BOOK

"Phew!" Harriet Plume sat down wearily on an old tree stump. She mopped her brow and looked at the small pile of wild crab apples she had collected in her basket.

"Not enough here to make me fat," she sighed. The peace of the wood was broken by excited squeaks as the Pollensnuff twins scampered through the trees.

"Quick Amy!" shrieked Pippin.
"This way!" They ran straight into Harriet,
nearly knocking her over.

Ripe crab apples spilled from their satchels.
"Whatever is going on?" Harriet cried.

"Please Mrs Plume," gasped Pippin,
"Sergeant Quilp is after us!"
"Oh, what shall we do?" squealed Amy.

Sergeant Quilp came stumbling through the brambles. "There you are, you young devils," he began. "Oh! Good morning Mrs Plume."

"Good morning Sergeant,"
said the squirrel. "What can I do for you?"
Amy and Pippin trembled behind her skirts.
"Well, I'd like a word with these two mice.
I've good reason to believe they have been
stealing Colonel Grunt's apples!"

"Ooh!" howled Pippin. Amy started to cry.
"Nonsense," said Harriet, "I'm sure
the twins wouldn't do that! There are
plenty growing wild in these woods.
You must be mistaken Sergeant."

Quilp scratched his head, puzzled.
"Well, if you say so Mrs Plume, but I
could have sworn I caught sight of them
up one of the Colonel's trees.

I suppose I might be wrong – mind,
if I catch these two scallywags
anywhere near his orchard again,
I'll tie their tails together!"
He stalked off, muttering to himself.

"Wow!" said Pippin. "That was close,
thank you Mrs Plume."
They were just about to run off,
but Harriet caught them both by the ear.

"Just a minute you two, not so fast,"
she said sternly. "You haven't really been
stealing apples have you?"

They hung their heads. "Why, I should
let you eat all these, and give yourselves
tummy-ache, just to teach you a lesson."

"We're very sorry," said Amy in a small voice. "They looked so delicious – much bigger than the wild ones – we just couldn't stop ourselves. Please, don't tell Colonel Grunt or Sergeant Quilp!"

"All right," answered Harriet,
"but you must make up for it."
"How Mrs Plume?" asked Pippin.
"You come home with me and find out!"

So they picked up all the apples and
followed Harriet Plume back to Acorns End.
Once inside her little kitchen, she gave
them both aprons. Pippin's was a frilly one,
and he looked so funny!

"You weigh the sugar," Harriet told him,
"and you, Amy, wash the apples.
We are going to repay the Colonel by
making him some crab apple jelly!"

They busied themselves,
squeaking all the time to each other.
Soon the water was boiling on the stove
and they watched Harriet chop up
the apples and put them in the pan.

"Now, you make some tea Amy,
while I give this a stir, and Pippin!
take your paws out
of the sugar bowl."

They all drank sweet blackberry leaf tea
and then Harriet put the crab apples into
a piece of muslin. She hung it from a hook
in the beam, where the juice slowly
dripped into a large bowl underneath.

Then she sent the twins to the garden shed
to find some large jars. "Bring them in,
and polish them until you can see your naught
little faces in them," said the squirrel.

They rushed off excitedly and, sure enough, tucked behind some sacks of grain they found several empty jars.

"Oooh!" cried Amy. A large black spider was crawling out of the jar she was carrying, and she almost dropped it.

Harriet boiled up the apple juice, mixed in the sugar and carefully poured it into the jars. "Can we try some now?" asked Pippin, smacking his lips.

"Certainly not," cried Harriet,
" you'll burn your tongue!
But while it cools I'll show you how
to make some pretty lids for the jars ."

When the crab apple jelly was set,
Harriet put three jars into her basket.
"Come along, we are taking these to
Mayfly Manor," she said. "And no
dipping into the jelly on the way!"

"Why, Mrs Plume, what have we here?"
asked Colonel Grunt as he opened the door.
Harriet told him how the twins
had helped her to make his favourite
jelly and he promptly asked them all
to join him for tea.

They sat down to little cups of
sweet chamomile tea,
thickly buttered oat-grass scones
and, of course, crab apple jelly.

"Mmm," sighed the Colonel.
He grinned at Harriet.
"Tell me twins, where *did* you find
such delicious crab apples?"